ESCAPE FROM
DAVY JONES

ESCAPE FROM DAVY JONES

By Jacqueline Ching
Based on characters created for the theatrical motion picture
"Pirates of the Caribbean: The Curse of the Black Pearl"
Screen Story by Ted Elliott & Terry Rossio and Stuart Beattie and Jay Wolpert
Screenplay by Ted Elliott & Terry Rossio
and characters created for the theatrical motion pictures
"Pirates of the Caribbean: Dead Man's Chest"
and "Pirates of the Caribbean: At World's End"
Written by Ted Elliott & Terry Rossio

New York

The *Black Pearl* charged through
the sea with Captain Jack Sparrow
at the helm.

Behind the ship, a monster called the Kraken was closing in.

The beast raised its tentacles,
ready to tear the ship in half.

With one hard pull on the sails,
Jack's crew crashed onto land.

The Kraken roared. Now the ship
was out of its reach.
"Bye-bye, beastie!" shouted Jack.

The *Flying Dutchman* appeared.
It was Davy Jones's ship.
The Kraken was Jones's pet.
Davy Jones was a man who had
turned into a creature.
Jack had made a deal with him.
Jack would have thirteen years
as captain, then he owed Davy Jones
his soul.

Jack counted.

Thirteen years weren't up yet.

Davy Jones's men pulled out
their weapons. Jack's crew had to fight.

The crew was attacked.

Jack knew that at any moment
Davy Jones himself would show up.
"Someone needs to defend
the beach!" he cried, jumping off
the ship. He knew Davy Jones
couldn't step on land.

"Someone needs to defend
the captain!" cried Jack's men.
Then they jumped off the ship, too.

Jack swam to the shore.
He was safe!

"Jones isn't after you,"
a crew member told Jack. "I heard
his men say that he wants
something that belongs to him."

"What does that have to do
with me?" Jack asked.
"Yeah!" another pirate agreed. "I
heard them talking, too.
And there is no stick with three
pointy things around here."

Jack sat up.
This stick sounded a lot like
a golden trident he had found
when he was a boy. Jack kept it
safe in his locker!

The only way to get Davy Jones
to go away was to return the trident
to him.

"Very well! We've got to go back
to the ship!" Jack said.

The men didn't move.

"All right! All right! I'll go by myself,"
Jack said.

Jack swam back to the *Pearl*.
The men didn't believe that
Jack would really give up his
treasure.

Jack went into his quarters and came out with a sack in his hand. He opened the sack and took something out.

Suddenly, Davy Jones appeared.
"Hello, Fish face!" Jack said.

"The trident! I knew you
would have it, Sparrow,"
Davy Jones said. "Give it to me!"

"First promise you'll
leave me alone," Jack said.

Davy Jones took the trident
and growled, "I make no promises.
And don't forget, you will soon
need to pay me your debt!"
Then Jones and his boat disappeared
under the sea.
Jack jumped off and swam to the *Pearl*.

The crew saw that Davy Jones
was gone.
They came back aboard Jack's ship.
"Captain!" said a sailor.
"We can't believe you gave up
your treasure!"

"I didn't give up anything," Jack said.
"But we saw you—" the younger
sailor began.

"A fancy pitchfork!" Jack said,
"**This** is what he was looking for!"
He held up the *real* trident.

Davy Jones figured out
that Jack had fooled him.
"Jack Sparrow!" he cried out.
Jack knew he would soon meet
Jones again.